For Amy, Landry, and Camille

MONKEY SEE, MONKEY DRAW

Alex Beard

Abrams Books for Young Readers, New York

At the foot of the Mbuno Hills in Africa,
a troop of monkeys lived in an old baobab tree.

They chattered and swung
from the branches and liked to play games.

The monkeys played Ring Around the Rhino.

They played Pin the Tail on the Warthog.

Their favorite game was Monkey in the Middle,

which they played with the last baobab nut from their ancient tree.

In the hills where the monkeys played, there was a cave.

It was very dark, and the monkeys never went inside.

One day, Elephant came to visit.
"Can I play?" he asked.

"Elephant in the Middle!" the monkeys cheered.

The monkeys tried to keep the baobab nut away from Elephant, but Elephant was too big.

He easily plucked the prize from the air.

Excited, Elephant launched the baobab nut.

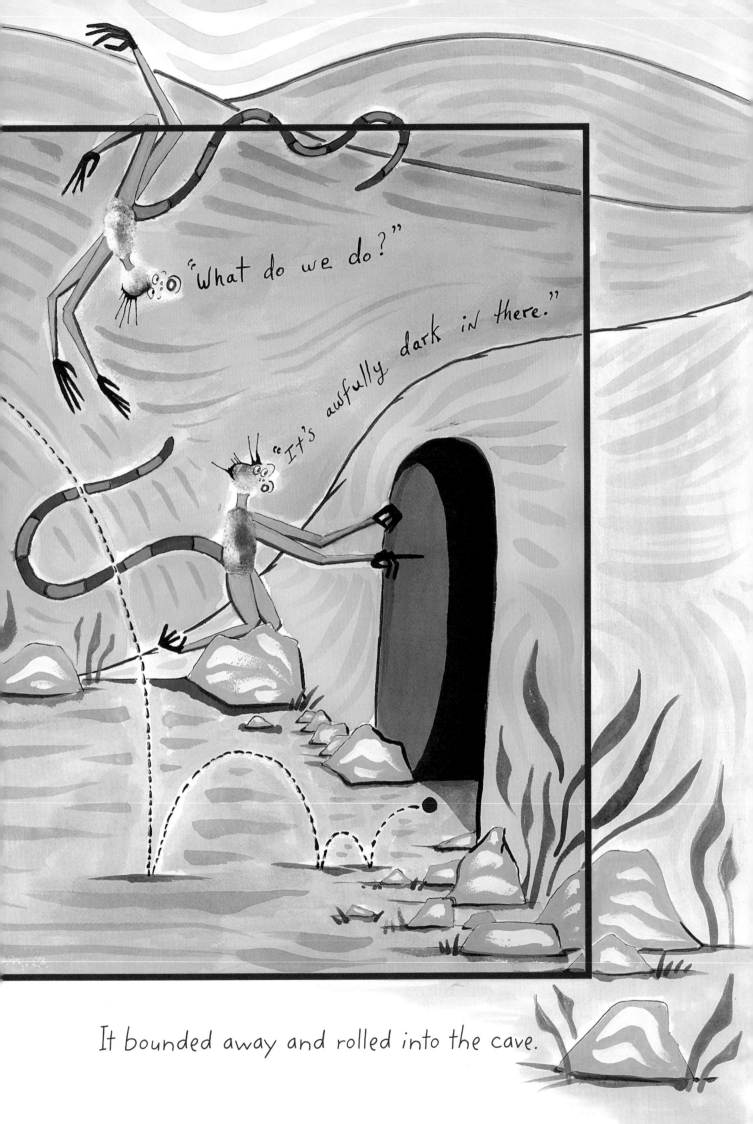

It bounded away and rolled into the cave.

"Silly monkeys," Elephant said. "Don't be afraid of the dark. Come with me and I'll show you there's nothing to fear."

With a few curious and brave monkeys clinging to his back, Elephant walked into the cave.

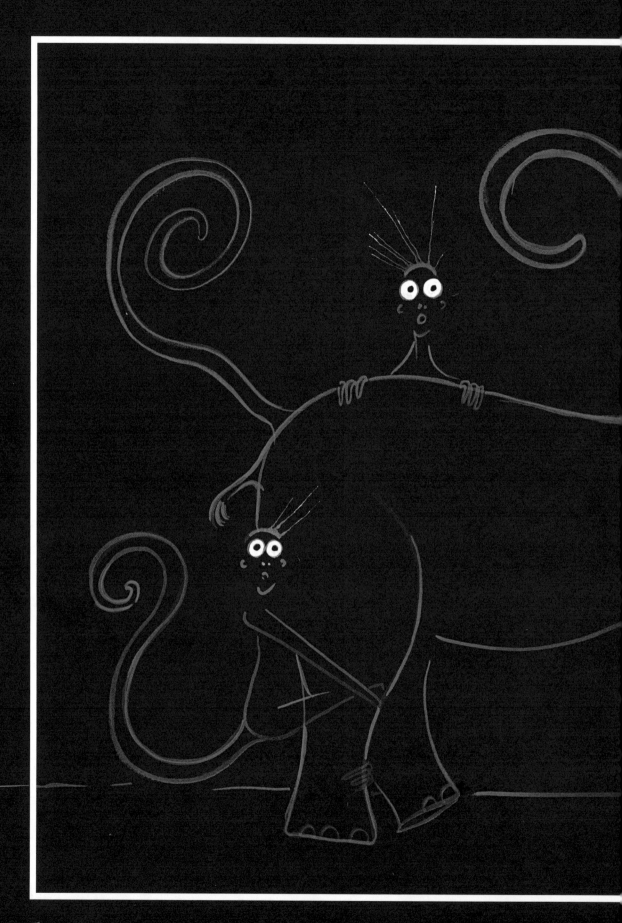

Inside, the cave was cool and musty.
It was hard for Elephant and the monkeys to see.

After a few moments, their eyes adjusted to the dark.

The walls of the cave were decorated
with paintings of animals.

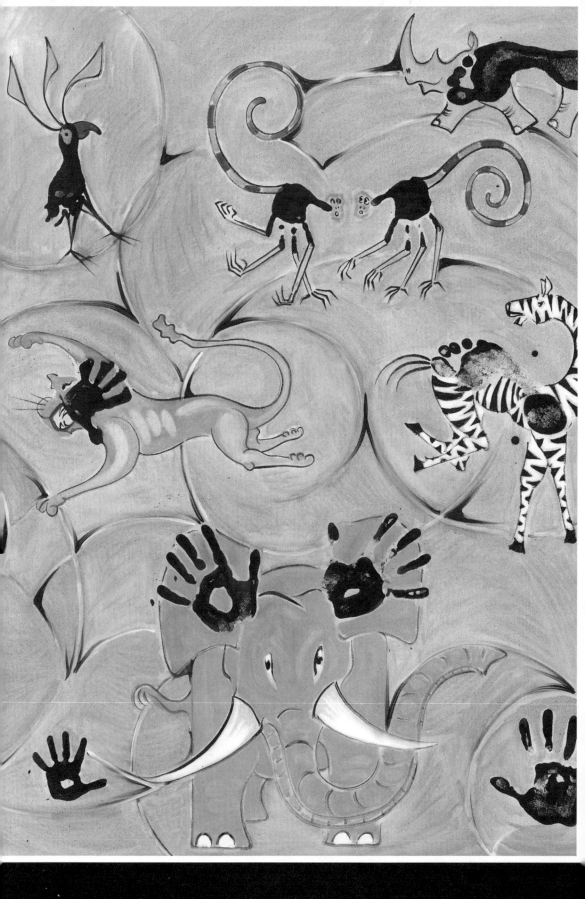

Each picture was made
from a handprint or footprint

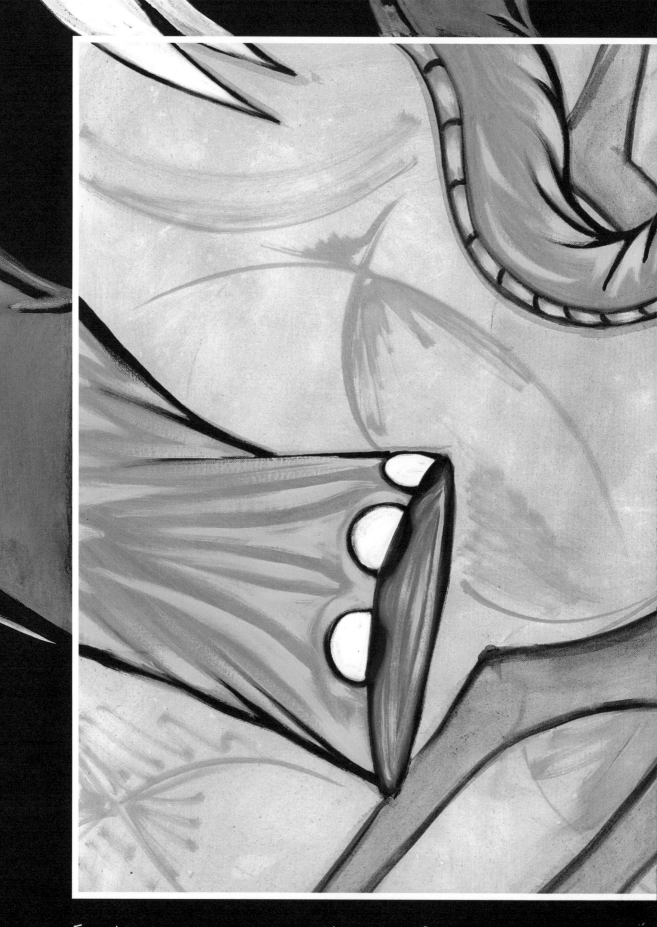

Elephant looked down at his own feet..
He stepped in a muddy corner
and pressed one foot against a clean spot on the wall.

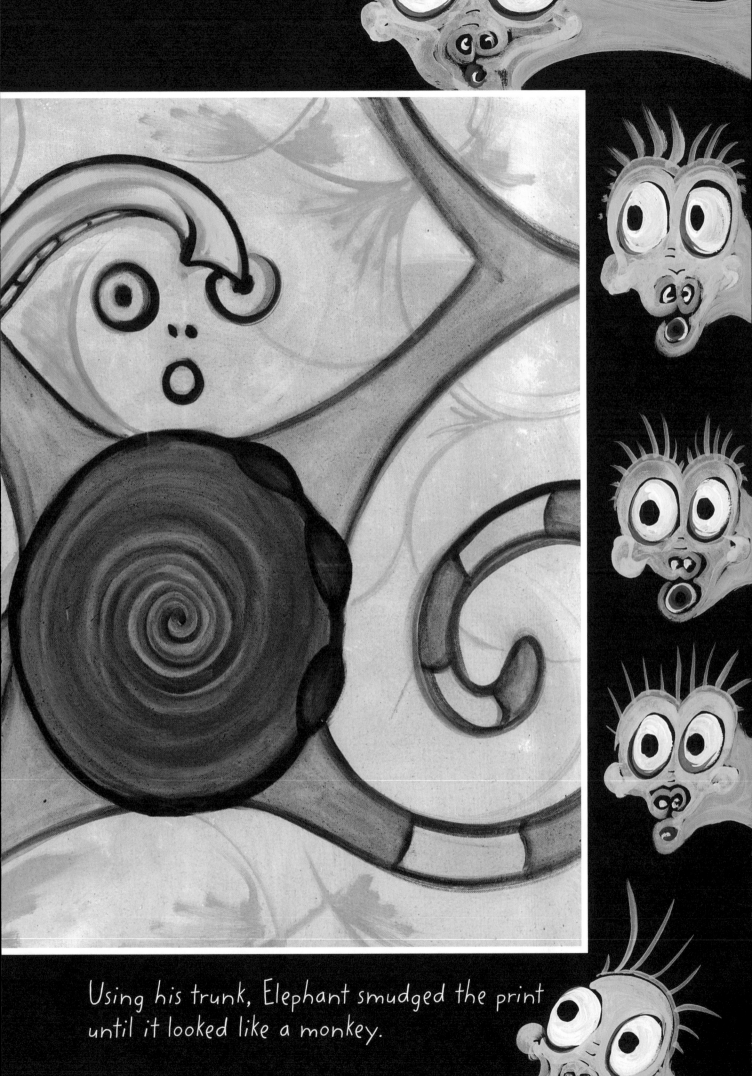

Using his trunk, Elephant smudged the print
until it looked like a monkey.

The monkeys were delighted.
They forgot their fear of the dark—and the lost nut.

Jumping up and down, they shrieked,
"A new game!"

The monkeys ran outside to show their friends.

They called this new game Monkey See, Monkey Draw.

Before long, a few monkeys bickered over whose painting was the best.

Soon, all the monkeys were arguing.

As the monkeys squabbled, it began to rain.

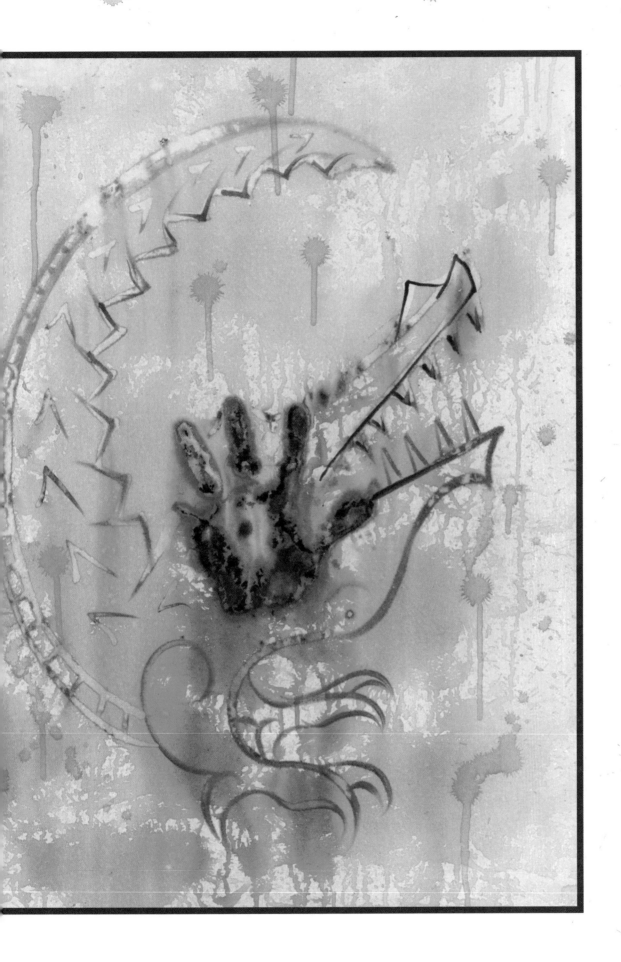

Their paintings dripped and ran
and turned back to mud.

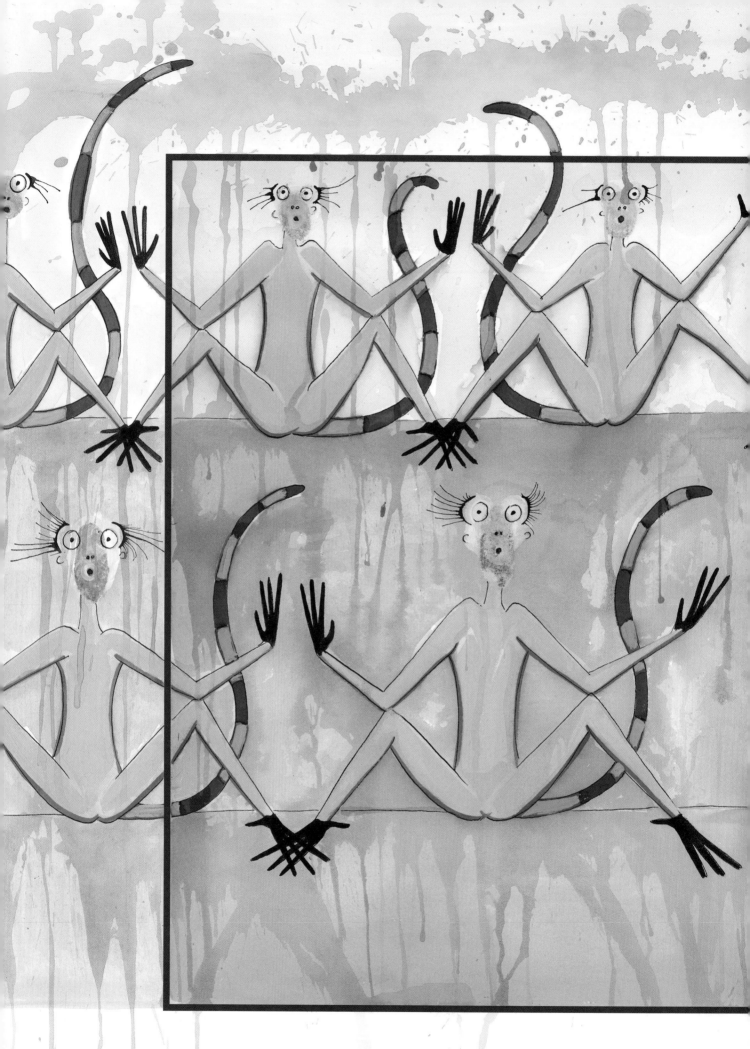

The monkeys sat in the rain.
"All our work is gone," they said.

"Whose painting was best? Who won the game?"

Elephant walked out of the cave with the lost baobab nut.

"No one is the winner," he said. "It's not a contest."

His feet covered in fresh mud, Elephant stomped down on a clean slate and started to draw.

The monkeys got up to join in. Soon, they were all laughing and painting in the sun.

The monkeys still live in the baobab tree, but they're no longer afraid of the dark painted cave.

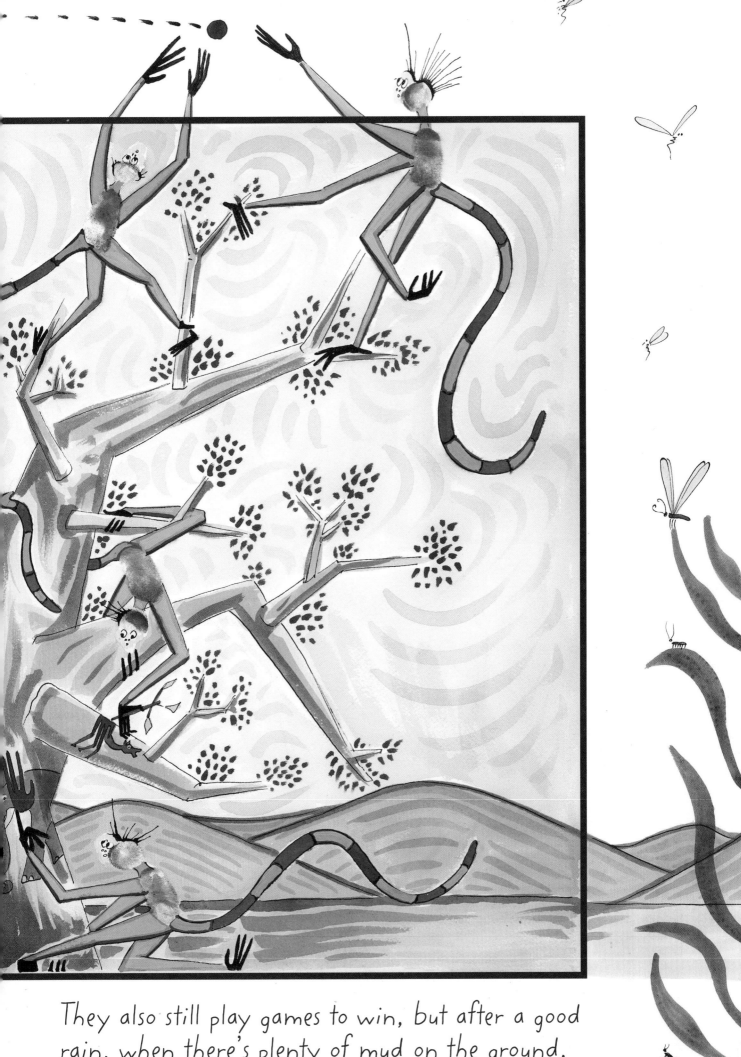

They also still play games to win, but after a good rain, when there's plenty of mud on the ground, they paint and draw just for fun.

Artists have used handprints as primary elements in their work since the beginning of time. From marks in the earliest cave paintings, to Native American decorations on horses' flanks, to symbols on the bodies of Aboriginal warriors preparing for battle, the handprint has been a constant through the ages. Today, we still teach children to begin their artistic endeavors by turning the outlines of their hands into turkeys at Thanksgiving.

My own hand- and footprint art began because my fingers are almost always covered in ink and paint. As a result, I tend to leave smudges behind (whether I want to or not) on just about everything I touch. As a chronic doodler, it didn't take very long for me to find something more recognizable in these remnants, which I could accentuate with a few lines to create whimsical works of art. In fact, every monkey in this book is made from my thumbprint!

Over the last few years, I have traveled the country, working with children to help encourage their creativity. Tracing a child's hand and turning the palm and fingers into the body, legs, and head of anything from a giraffe to a butterfly to a horse—and of course a monkey—fascinates the kids. It gives them an easy starting place from which to make their own works of art, and it helps them think beyond their immediate comfort zone of flowers, rockets, and square houses with triangular roofs and stick-figure families. Just as important, I have been delighted to find that making hand- and footprint art is something that children can do with their parents, engaging the older generations with the younger

in an exercise that is both fun and creative. To prove the point, the cave paintings in this book were made from my hands and feet and those of my four-year-old son. The morning we went to my studio to work together was one of the best days I can remember, and is an event that my boy still talks about all the time.

As far as choosing monkeys as the protagonists for this story, that decision was easy. I happen to love monkeys. When I was younger, I became friends with of a pair of vervet monkeys in Africa named Radio and Mbili. I have a particularly fond place in my heart for them, as they were the most loyal, funny, and cute companions, even though Mbili bit me a few times. (I have the scars on my knee to prove it.) Finally, I think monkeys are the members of the animal kingdom that we can most easily relate to, and like me,

most children seem to love them. That love is something that stays with us for a lifetime. Just think of how many parents call their kids "our little monkeys" with nothing but affection.

Hopefully, children will read this story, associate themselves with the troop in the baobab tree, and learn to have fun with art, understanding that, just like the squabbling monkeys learned in the story, it should be enough to simply enjoy art and the process of creating it in the first place.

The illustrations in this book were made
with pen and ink and watercolor on paper.

Library of Congress Cataloging-in-Publication Data

Beard, Alex, 1970–
Monkey see, monkey draw / by Alex Beard.
p. cm.
Summary: Elephant leads a troop of monkeys into a cave they have been afraid to explore,
and after admiring the paintings found on the walls they make their own art with mud,
squabbling over whose painting is best until Elephant explains that this is not a game to win
or lose.
ISBN 978-0-8109-8970-2
[1. Play—Fiction. 2. Competition (Psychology)—Fiction. 3. Monkeys—Fiction. 4.
Elephants—Fiction. 5. Africa—Fiction.] I. Title.
PZ7.B3688Mon 2010
[E]—dc22
2009039448

Book design by Chad W. Beckerman

Printed and bound in Hong Kong, China
10 9 8 7 6 5 4 3 2 1

Abrams Books for Young Readers are available at special discounts when purchased
in quantity for premiums and promotions as well as fundraising or educational
use. Special editions can also be created to specification. For details, contact
specialmarkets@abramsbooks.com or the address below.

ABRAMS
THE ART OF BOOKS SINCE 1949

115 West 18th Street
New York, NY 10011
www.abramsbooks.com

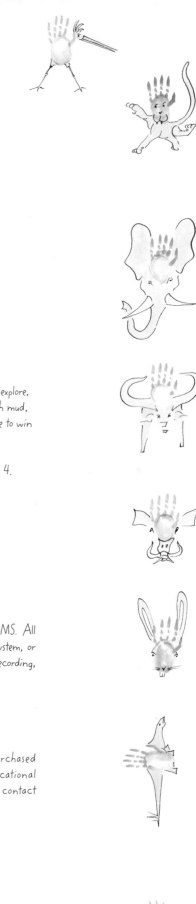